Lucky Mucky Pup

bzzz

For Hogan and Tamara

First published in hardback in Great Britain by Andersen Press Ltd in 1999
First published in paperback in Great Britain by Collins Picture Books in 2001

1 3 5 7 9 10 8 6 4 2

ISBN: 0 00 664759 6

Text and illustrations copyright © Ken Brown 1999

The HarperCollins website address is: www.fireandwater.com

Printed and bound in Hong Kong

Lucky Mucky Pup

Written and illustrated by
Ken Brown

Collins
An imprint of HarperCollins*Publishers*

Mucky Pup was snoozing in the sun
when a bee buzzed by.

He snapped at it.

He jumped at it.

He pounced at it.

But the bee buzzed on…

So Mucky Pup chased it –
into the vegetable garden…

WHOOOPS

bzzz

and into the farmyard.

"Come on, Pig!" he called.
"Come and chase this bee with me!"

past the shed and around the pond

and into the meadow.

bbbbzzzzzbbbzbbbbbzzzbbbzzzzzzzzzzz

"Where's that bee gone now?"
panted Mucky Pup.
"To fetch his friends," gasped Pig. "Look!"
Mucky Pup looked and…Uh-oh!

And how they ran! Out of the meadow…

past the shed and across
the pond…

back to the barn

and under the hay,

down the hill and into…

SPLAT!

…the farmyard,

into the garden and under the washing,
safe and sound!
     But…

"Mucky Pup! What have you been doing?"
wailed the farmer's wife.

"Poor Mucky Pup. *He's* not to blame," cried the children.
"He was being chased by that swarm of bees."

"Well, he's lucky they didn't catch him," said their mum.
"Come on, Mucky Pup,
let's clean you up."

So, instead of getting a scolding, Mucky Pup had a bath under the garden hose. And that was *much* more fun. Lucky Mucky Pup!

Lucky Mucky Pup is the third book about this adorable puppy. In the first title, *Mucky Pup*, everyone thinks he's just too mucky to play with, except the equally mucky Pig! In *Mucky Pup's Christmas*, Mucky Pup spoils the preparations and gets in trouble. But when the snow falls, he is forgiven, and finds that Christmas is lots of fun after all!

'Deliciously boisterous'.   *Junior Education*

Ken Brown's Mucky Pup series has proved a tremendous success. It has found fans all over the world amongst children who love to get mucky like their endearing hero, and has been translated into eleven different languages.